BE A BRIDGE

Irene Latham and **Charles Waters**

illustrated by **Nabila Adani**

Carolrhoda Books
Minneapolis

With love and gratitude to Alonso, Ernesto, and Michele —I.L.

For Amani, Gabriella, Ben, Dane, Brielle, and Brooke Lynn.
I'm proud to be your uncle! —C.W.

For Mba Pam, Hillary, Tom, and Emily —N.A.

Carolrhoda Books®
An imprint of Lerner Publishing Group, Inc.
241 First Avenue North
Minneapolis, MN 55401 USA

For reading levels and more information, look up this title at www.lernerbooks.com.

Designed by Kimberly Morales.
Main body text set in Mikado. Typeface provided by HVD Fonts.
The illustrations in this book were digitally created with Photoshop.

Library of Congress Cataloging-in-Publication Data

Names: Latham, Irene, author. | Waters, Charles, 1973- author. | Adani, Nabila, 1991- illustrator.
Title: Be a bridge / Irene Latham and Charles Waters ; illustrated by Nabila Adani.
Description: Minneapolis : Carolrhoda Books, [2022] | Includes bibliographical references. | Audience: Ages 4–9 | Audience: Grades K–1 | Summary: "Upbeat rhyming verse and colorful illustrations of a diverse group of students invite readers to "be a bridge" by taking actions that foster inclusivity, respect, and connection" —Provided by publisher.
Identifiers: LCCN 2021051167 (print) | LCCN 2021051168 (ebook) | ISBN 9781728423388 (library binding) | ISBN 9781728460758 (ebook)
Subjects: CYAC: Stories in rhyme. | Behavior—Fiction. | Kindness—Fiction. | Respect—Fiction. | LCGFT: Stories in rhyme.
Classification: LCC PZ8.3.L3443 Be 2022 (print) | LCC PZ8.3.L3443 (ebook) | DDC [E]—dc23

LC record available at https://lccn.loc.gov/2021051167
LC ebook record available at https://lccn.loc.gov/2021051168

Manufactured in the United States of America
1-49167-49308-12/21/2021

Love is the bridge between you and everything.
—Rumi

When you wake up
to a world of bad news,
pack up your backpack
and lace up your shoes.

You've got a job to do—
BE A BRIDGE.

When someone new walks in,

be the first to say hello.
Your smile could be the sunshine
that helps a friendship grow.

If you see someone outside the circle watching others play,

wave them over, invite them in—
if they say no, that's okay.

When a classmate teases another
for how they look or behave,

say, "Hey you, stop being rude!"
Standing up to others is brave.

If your neighbor at the lunch table
bows their head in prayer,
make sure to give them space—
there's room for respect everywhere.

When a friend's mood turns stormy
over a mistake made in art,
saying, "That's happened to me before,"
is a great place to start.

When all the swings are taken
and your feelings turn to stone—
remember a bridge stays steady.
It's all right to be alone.

When someone else is speaking,
pay attention to their words.
Listening takes courage.
Let every voice be heard.

When a classmate's face is
in their hands
and there's nothing you can say,

simply share a quiet moment—
being present helps in its own way.

When the school day comes to an end,
look to the sky and sun.

Know others are building bridges.
You're not the only one.

BE A BRIDGE
from fear to trust.

BE A BRIDGE
between them and us.

RAINBOW SHOELACES

A bridge is love.
And love is you!
Take a chance—
imagine all the good you can do.

AUTHORS' NOTE

This book started with two pairs of rainbow shoelaces. We wrote a book together called *Can I Touch Your Hair? Poems of Race, Mistakes, and Friendship*. During events and at author visits to schools, we gave away rainbow shoelaces as a symbol of our book's messages about identity and inclusivity. (The LGBTQIA+ community uses rainbows in a similar way.) We often wore our own rainbow shoelaces to book events, and sometimes readers wore them too! The experience got us thinking of our younger selves, and how if we really had met in elementary school, we might have worn rainbow shoelaces and formed a sort of social justice team. And *that* sparked the idea for this picture book.

We wrote many, MANY drafts that didn't quite hit the mark we were aiming for. It wasn't until we found the "bridge" metaphor (thank you, Alonso, Ernesto, and Michele!) that the book you're holding in your hands came to be. A rainbow is a bridge made of light and water—and makes us think of our hopes for the world. Bridges made of steel, wood, and other solid materials are steady, and they connect us to one another. We realized what we need—and what we want to be—are bridges.

Books can be bridges too. Here at I & C Construction Co., we build bridges with words. We're grateful to Carol Hinz and Shaina Olmanson and her son Magnus for helping us construct this book. Thanks also to Ann Marie Corgill for sharing her compliments circle expertise!

We're learning every day how to love the world better by reaching out to others, being better listeners, and keeping our hearts open. Even though it can be tough sometimes—like when we feel shy or don't want to risk getting in trouble or worry we won't be supported—it's still important to try. We can ask others for help. Help might come from a parent or other caregiver, an older sibling, a teacher, a trusted neighbor, or someone else in your life who supports you. Sometimes it's the smallest actions that make all the difference in a person's experience. So go ahead: be a bridge!

BRIDGE BUILDER ACTIVITIES

Build a Bridge with Everyday Items
http://jdaniel4smom.com/2016/08/stem-activity-build-bridge-everyday-items.html

Build a Popsicle Stick and Duct Tape Bridge
https://preschooltoolkit.com/blog/craft-stick-bridge-for-toy-cars/

Compliments Chain
A paper variation of the Compliments Circle (below), this activity invites students to write a compliment about a classmate on a slip of paper. Use tape, a glue stick, or a stapler to link the slips into a chain. Hang the compliment chain in the classroom as a visible reminder of kindnesses shared.

Compliments Circle
Gather children in a circle on the floor. Have one child start by sharing a compliment about the person beside them. That person says, "thank you"; gives a high five; turns to the next person; and shares a compliment about them. Continue until the first child receives a compliment.

Create Empathy Bands
https://www.teacher2teacher.education/2019/04/04/3-creative-ways-to-build-empathy-in-the-classroom/

Listen First, Speak Later
Pair children and give them a topic for discussion. One child will be the speaker, and the other will be the listener. After the speaker shares their views (without interruption), the listener shares two things they heard. Then the speaker and the listener change roles.

Listen to "Rainbow Connection"
Play a recording of this song by Paul Williams and Kenneth Ascher. Ask children these questions: What are your wishes for the world? What can you do to make that dream come true?

MORE BOOKS FOR BUILDING BRIDGES

Choi, Yangsook. *The Name Jar.* Illustrated by Yangsook Choi. New York: Knopf, 2001.

Erskine, Kathryn. *All of Us.* Illustrated by Alexandra Boiger. New York: Philomel, 2021.

Faruqi, Reem. *I Can Help.* Illustrated by Mikela Prevost. Grand Rapids, MI: Eerdmans, 2021.

Feder, Tyler. *Bodies Are Cool.* New York: Dial, 2021.

Paul, Baptiste, and Miranda Paul. *Peace.* Illustrated by Estelí Meza. New York: NorthSouth, 2021.

Wilson, Diane, Sun Yung Shin, Shannon Gibney, and John Coy. *Where We Come From.* Illustrated by Dion MBD. Minneapolis: Carolrhoda Books, 2022.

Woodson, Jacqueline. *The Day You Begin.* Illustrated by Rafael López. New York: Nancy Paulsen Books, 2018.

BRIDGE BUILDER PLEDGE

I will be the one to reach out and say hello.

I will keep an open mind.

I will give my full attention when someone is speaking to make them feel seen, heard, and valued.

I will acknowledge other people's feelings.

I will offer encouragement instead of criticism.

I will talk positively about others.

I will invite everyone to be part of an activity.

I will flex my empathy muscles and try to understand another's viewpoint.

I will be myself.

I will use computer and phone screens to strengthen connections with others.

I will not interrupt a comfortable silence.

I will give myself time for rest and reflection.

_____

My Name

Download and print copies of this pledge at qrs.lernerbooks.com/beabridge.